# DOGDUNNIT

## PETER BENTLY   TOR FREEMAN

Andersen Press

**Inspector Keyhole** wore a frown.
A night of crime had swept the town.

First published in Great Britain in 2024 by Andersen Press Ltd.,

20 Vauxhall Bridge Road, London SW1V 2SA, UK.

Vijverlaan 48, 3062 HL Rotterdam, Nederland.

Text copyright © Peter Bently 2024. Illustration copyright © Tor Freeman 2024.

1   3   5   7   9   10   8   6   4   2

British Library Cataloguing in Publication Data available. ISBN 978 1 83913 181 3

FSC
www.fsc.org

MIX
Paper from
responsible sources
FSC® C104723

Who chewed the rug?

Who trashed the chair?

Who scattered rubbish everywhere?

Tore Katie's favourite
jeans to shreds?

Left muddy paw prints on the beds?

Who blocked the loo with
Grandad's slippers?

Who scoffed the sausages
and kippers?

Who sent a vase of flowers flying –
just where Mummy's phone was lying?

And who did a doo-doo,
small and neat,
that Daddy stood on –
in bare feet?

The great detective **Purrlock Jones**
Said, "I feel it in my bones.
It's **MOGGIARTY's** work, it's plain.
The **King of Crime** has struck again!"

**Inspector Keyhole** shook his head.
"It's **DOGS** what's done these crimes," he said.
"**It wasn't us!**" the dogs protested –

But **Keyhole** had them all arrested.

**Purrlock** watched and made a vow:
"I'll prove that **Keyhole's** wrong – but how?
**Aha!**" she said. "What's this I've found?
A **mouse's paw prints** on the ground!"

Soon the **dogs** all stood, dismayed,
Wearing **paw-cuffs** on parade.

**Big** and **small**
and **long** and **short**
Were led before the judge in court.

"It wasn't me!" cried Toby Pug.
"I did not trash the brand new rug!
We dogs would never do such crimes.
At least," he said, "not many times."

His Honour **Mister Justice Mogg**
Looked down severely at each dog.

"**You're guilty!**

It's as plain as day.

**Lock** these **CRIMINALS** away!"

Then **Purrlock Jones** burst into sight,
Crying, "**STOP!**" with all her might.
She said, "This mouse knows who's to blame!
**Nibbler Watson** is her name."

"Every night," declared the mouse,
"I like to **ramble** through each house
To check in all the floorboard cracks
For crumbs of **cheese** and other **snacks**.

Last night I saw a **rascal creeping**
While the dogs were soundly **sleeping**!
Everybody take a look
At these **videos** I took."

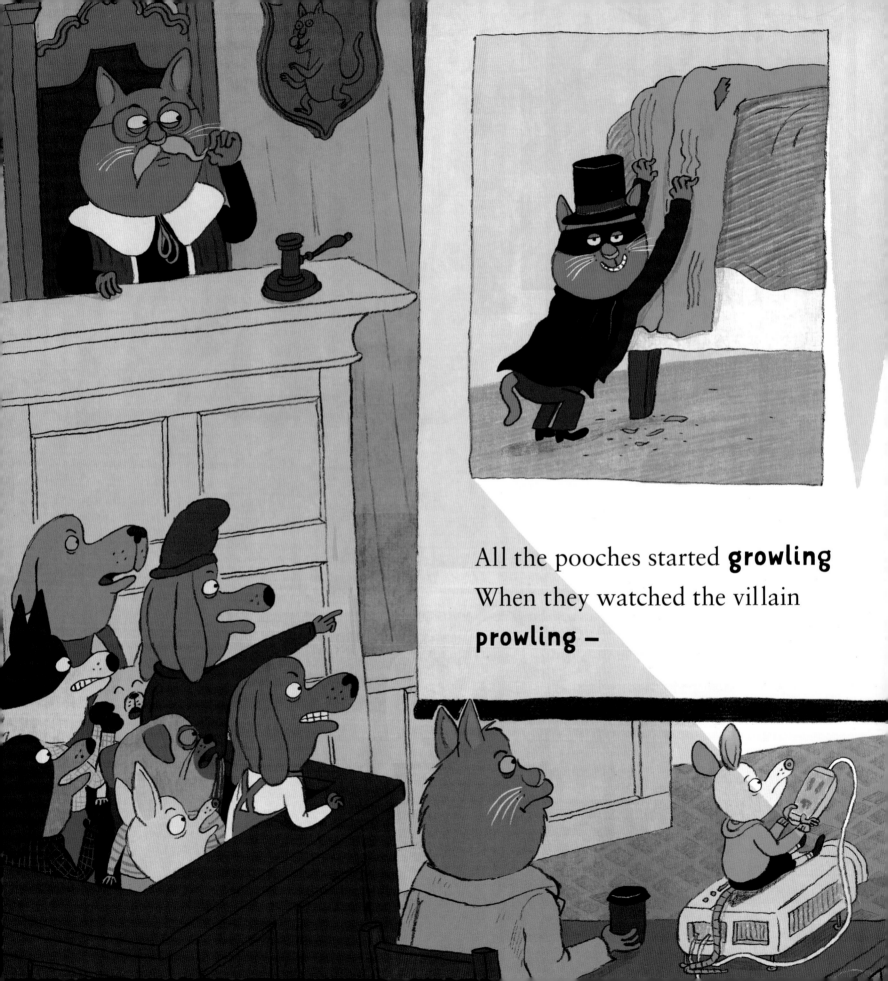

All the pooches started **growling**
When they watched the villain
**prowling** –

And tearing **Katie's jeans** to shreds!
Leaving **paw prints** on the beds!
**Stealing** sausages and kippers!
Blocking up the loo with **slippers!**

Scattering sacks of stinky trash!
Sending vases flying – **SMASH!**

And – most terrible of all –
Doing a **doo-doo** in the hall!

The dogs went wild. "**We told you so!**
We're **innocent!** Please **let us go!!**"
The judge cried, "**No!** These films are **fake**.
The dogs are **guilty**, no mistake!"

But **Purrlock** said, "There's one last scene.
**Everybody watch the screen!**"

The mouse went on, "The **night** was **dark**.
I tracked that **baddie** through the **park** ...

And saw him **slip in** through a flap,
Remove his mask, and take **a nap**."

"**Good grief!**" cried **Keyhole**. "I was wrong.
It was **MOGGIARTY** all along!"

"Thanks," said **Purrlock** with a bow.
"But where is **MOGGIARTY** now?
That cunning **master of disguise**,
Is **right** before our
very **eyes!**

Who wants to **lock** up **every dog?** Who else but –

"Mister Justice MOGG!"

The culprit cried,

"You can't catch me!"

He tried to **flee**, but didn't see
The **mouse's tail**,
which made him **trip**,
**Stumble, tumble,
slide** and **slip**

Into the **arms** of **Sergeant Dawes**,

Who boomed, "**You're nicked!**"
to great applause.

"**Well done, Watson!**" **Purrlock** cried.
"**Don't mention it!**" the mouse replied.

As the crook was led away
He hissed, "I'll be revenged one day!
Though **Purrlock Jones** has won this time
No jail can hold the **King of Crime**,

And as white is white and black is black –
**MOGGIARTY** will be back!"